Honey Moon

By Harlowe Frost

Coastal Wolves

1: Pacific Pack

2: Wolf Magic

4: Campus Prowl

4: Loan Wolf

5: Pack Triage

6: Mystical Science

7: Lupine Investigation

7.5: Honey Moon

Dedication:

I want to thank Angela Grimes. She is the goofiest person I know. She'll read all my books helping to add detail, depth, and help to reach into my mind and bring out what I'm thinking. I want to thank Weslee Imrisek. They are the best editor I know. They are also a wonderful friend, who is there to listen to any of my thoughts, worries, or random babbling. I want to thank Nicole Maness (and wife) who read all my words as soon as I write them and make me laugh at their antics. And of course I want to thank my family who support my writing, even when they don't understand it.

Chapter 1 – Travel

"Sleep during travel isn't really sleep, is it?" Paige groused. They stood in a parking garage at the airport in Paris ... *the* Paris, the one in France.

Tamsin waggled her eyebrows at her now wife. A tiny thrill tickled her at the thought, even as tired as she was. "Why do you think I scheduled our trip as a red eye? Leave Chicago at nearly nine pm, arrive in Paris at eleven-thirty in the morning their time, and spend the day acclimating to their time zone ... genius if you think about it. Pure brilliance."

Paige sighed. "It *was* nice to visit Chicago again, see the people we'd befriended during the few months we lived here."

Tamsin smiled at Paige. "The pack wanted to throw a small celebration for us. Who was I to deny them?"

"You didn't have to tell them I'd spent the last two months trying to learn French!" As they stood in the parking structure waiting for their driver's Tesla to update, Tamsin saw Paige's cheeks color. Her wife ... *wife!* ... tried to glare at her, but then the fun-loving woman laughed. "I can't believe they had a native speaker in their pack. Did you see his face when I said, 'Je voudrais un café et un croissant.'? I thought he'd run and wash his ears out!"

"Or dump his gin and tonic in them to sanitize them!" Tamsin chuckled. "Everyone got a good laugh from that."

Their driver popped out of the car. "Un café? You like before I drop you off? It will be another fifteen minutes. I am sorry. This is a new car for me." His accent was thick, but his English was understandable.

"No worries." Tamsin replied. "We don't have any plans until tomorrow."

"Merci."

Once they got on the road, the trip from the airport to their hotel, Hotel Les Theatres, took upwards of an hour and a half.

The Parisian drivers were fearless. Tamsin had spent years driving in downtown Chicago, but she wasn't sure she could keep up with the chaos of what she saw in the tight streets and the mysterious dance of cars in this foreign city. Outside her window, the other cars were within inches—centimeters—of her window, and they were all driving at speed.

At several points, emergency vehicles sounded from behind. The first time, both she and Paige checked out the window behind them. Their driver smiled. "Oh, it is not like how it is for you Americans, we don't stop. We just let the vehicle pass when it catches up with us."

Paige's head bounced from the emergency vehicle to the driver. "Do you know much about our ways?"

The driver smiled back at her. "I lived in New York for five years, working with my uncle in construction. Driving there was like a stroll in the park, very nice."

Tamsin snorted. She wouldn't have believed New York traffic would be considered peaceful before being driven in the circus of Paris.

The hotel was on a side street. Inside, the entrance wall was covered in theater posters. Tired and a bit grumpy, Paige went to check them in. She mumbled something about needing coffee, and the lovely receptionist asked, "Espresso or long?"

Eyes as wide as saucers, Paige said, "Espresso, double, ah ... merci."

Tamsin grinned. "Deux, s'il vous plaîs."

The receptionist waved them over to some low, red velvet chairs and brought them their drinks. Once they'd had their delicious start to the day—at noon local time, three a.m. California time—they got the keys to their room and headed up.

The room was filled with a king size bed, but that was about it. If they moved sideways, they could just make their way around it. On one side of the bed was a small desk, the other an open closet. Behind the headboard was the split bathroom. The toilet on one side, the shower and sink on the other.

"Small," Tamsin muttered to herself. "Everything is small."

Flopping on the bed, she pulled out her phone and searched the immediate area. Tamsin found a yoga establishment across the street that also sold coffee. "How about I go get bigger caffeines, and then we can explore."

Paige, down for the count and sprawled on the bed, merely nodded.

Tamsin scooted into the tiny elevator, about the size of her and Paige with their luggage, and saw the sign that stated it fit seven people. She laughed and remembered on the way in that the driver noted everything in Paris was 'small.' So far, she hadn't seen anything to dispute that.

In the shop, Tamsin took a moment to enjoy the smell of fresh-baked pastries and brewing coffee. The familiar scents warmed her to her soul. There were a few people sitting at the tables scattered inside and along the sidewalk. Most were on laptops. The few words she heard spoken were in French and she didn't understand any of it.

The woman behind the counter switched to English when she approached. Since arriving in Paris, most people had. Tamsin tried her French. "Deux croissants chocolate, s'il vous plaît."

The woman smiled. "Actually, a croissant is just the plain one. This is 'pain de chocolate.'"

"Really? That's interesting. It isn't as common to eat in America."

"Oh? You don't have them often?"

Tamsin chuckled. "No. I may have a pain de chocolate or even a croissant once or twice a year, but not more often than that. Others may go for them more regularly, but I don't think so."

The woman seemed intrigued by that. Once she handed Tamsin her treats, Tamsin headed back to the hotel.

Before they'd left Santa Cruz, a friend had given them some ideas of where they could eat in town. Most places were nice dinner spots. She and Paige decided to head out and walk. Being mid-June, the weather was beautiful—not a cloud in the sky. Apparently they weren't the only ones who thought so. The area was full of people. Between them and their wolves, they felt safe, always aware of the people around them. They were near a promenade with stores on either side, no cars. They walked for about a mile and a half.

They stopped at La Baguette Du Relais. Inside, there was a woman talking to the server in French. Once done, the woman behind the counter turned to them. "Can I help you?" Tamsin thought she could listen to the French accent for hours.

Amusement bubbled in Tamsin as Paige's face scrunched up in disappointment. Paige sighed. "It's obvious we speak English?"

The woman shrugged. "Oui?"

Tamsin pointed at the display. "Two sandwiches with a side of fries."

"How would you like the meat? Rare, medium, or well done?"

Paige made a hungry sound. "Medium-rare, oh, wait, um, rare please."

The woman's eyes sparkled. "How French!" *No, how werewolf.* The woman continued as Tamsin had her silly thought. "And to drink?"

On the counter were small globes of wine. Paige pointed. "Two of these."

After they ordered, they found a seat out on the sidewalk and people-watched. Paige's eyes widened. "People here are so much more fashionable than back home."

Tamsin nodded. "But there are so many smokers. It's wild."

Once the food was delivered, they both dug in. The steak sandwich with a house sauce and fries was fantastic. The last two meals had been in the airport and on the plane. This one was amazing. After they ate, they headed home ... well, hotel. Paige pointed to a crepe shop. "You know, it's probably illegal to *not* get crepes at least once while we're here."

Tamsin snorted. "You just want Nutella." Before they could move on, the romantic nature of the city overcame her, and she wrapped Paige in her arms and kissed her in the middle of the street. Around them, people went about their day, but Tamsin savored their moment of near perfection.

Paige pulled away and laughed. "You're not distracting me that easily. I do want Nutella, *wife*. But I think what I said is *also* true."

Tamsin almost swooned when she heard the word, 'wife' practically shouted to the heavens. "Fine, let's go find some dessert before we're escorted from France."

They headed in. On the first board were savory options. But then they found the ones they wanted, fruits and sugars. Paige got Nutella and cookies and cream. Tamsin ordered caramel and strawberries. Despite the heat of the day and the sugar overload, they enjoyed the sweet goodness.

After that, they made their way back to their hotel. It was time to admit sleep was a real need.

Chapter 2 – Early to Bed ...

Tamsin woke and gazed at her beautiful wife. She leaned over to give Paige a quick kiss to wake her up.

With a low moan, Paige curled her arms around Tamsin's neck and deepened the kiss. After a few moments, she pulled back. "I can get used to the city of love ... my love."

Tamsin rubbed up against her wife ... *wife!* ... and kissed down to her ear. "As much as I want to continue, we have about twenty minutes until we're going to be picked up by the tour service."

Paige made a disappointed sound before rolling away to slide out of bed. She showed off her lovely ass...ets before heading to the bathroom for a quick shower and to dress.

Breakfast service at the hotel started at seven. Their cab for the day of tours was scheduled to arrive at seven-ten. Despite the early morning, they still got a mug of coffee and a quick plate of chocolate croissants—pain de chocolate—before they were off! They had to get to the meeting spot for the morning at Giverny and afternoon at Versailles at seven forty-five. Being late wasn't an option.

They were part of a tour with ten other people. Their driver dropped them off, and the man who was part of the tour company pointed them towards a bus. Sitting, they waited. Behind them was a woman traveling by herself. Paige turned. "Hi! I'm Paige."

The other woman smiled wide. "I'm Sarah." Her British accent thrilled Tamsin. She was excited for their trip to London.

"Are you here alone?"

The woman nodded. "My partner is back home. He wasn't interested in Versailles. You?"

Paige's eyes widened and she leaned towards the other woman. "We're on our honeymoon."

"Oh! Congrats! Tell me about the ceremony. I love hearing a good story."

The two started talking as the small bus took off. Tamsin enjoyed listening as she relaxed in the bus seat. The ride down to Giverny, the private gardens of Monet, took a little over an hour.

Once there, the tour guide seemed to know everything. The gardens were beautiful but crowded. She had to rein in and set up extra blocks with her wolf, similar to when she'd gone to the airport. She hadn't planned on that for a simple outing.

The garden featured large, bright flowers, paths with low-hanging tree branches speckled with leaves and small flowers, and a small lake with a picturesque bridge across it.

Paige sighed. "I kind of wish she knew a bit less. We have thirty minutes to view the inside of Monet's house, get through the gift shop, and then back to the bus. The line into the house is a mile long—"

"Kilometer," Tamsin corrected Paige, as she ranted.

"What?"

"We're in France. Kilometer. And, since you said mile, probably a kilometer and a half."

As they spoke, the sky began to open up. The density of the crowd intensified as people pulled out umbrellas, the sidewalk dust got speckled with drops of rain, and Tamsin began to get wet.

Paige rolled her eyes. "Whatever, fine, a kilometer and a half, and it's starting to rain! So, metric woman, what do we do? Do we wait in the line with all the kids? Do we get the gifts I so want to buy? What?" She gazed around and then gestured, eyes wide. "The line for the bathroom is equally as long as well. I swear, travel is defined by the number of queues you stand in."

Tamsin sighed. "Probably the gift shop first, if that's what you really want, then check on the time. I loved the gardens, but all those people. I mean,

I'd love to see the house, but I came to see the gardens." She rubbed her hands up and down Paige's arms, hoping the contact would help calm her mate. As Paige's eyes softened, Tamsin gave her a quick kiss. She couldn't help it. With such beauty, no one would be able to resist. "I agree about the tour guide. She knew everything—which was fantastic—but my mind is spinning, and we don't have any time. By the time we leave Versailles, we'll know more history than the locals."

They headed into the gift shop and Tamsin watched as Paige's eyes grew. They left with a couple of notebooks, reusable bags, and a book on Monet's art.

The next stop was a three-course meal with wine.

The drive from Giverny to the restaurant was along country roads barely as wide as two cars. The tour bus they were in sped down the center of the road, only moving over when another car approached. At times, the road narrowed to one car width and if there was an oncoming car, it was a matter of letting one car go at a time.

They turned down a small, winding path and came to what appeared to be an old watermill. Inside, they were seated at an antique table. They ended up sitting with Sarah again. The three of them were becoming a unit for the day. In the center of the table stood tall glass bottles. In one was water, and the other two held red and white wine.

At each seat, the first course had been pre-set: a fish pate, made up of three kinds of fish, with a type of gelee at the top. On the side was a salad. *I don't know about fish Jell-o, but this is a fancy restaurant.* She smiled at her table-mates before digging in. It was interesting. Not bad, but very different.

Paige sipped some red wine. "You know, this is not as bad as it looks."

Sarah snorted. "Right. When we first sat down, I thought it would be atrocious. I know this is a fancy eatery, but it looks ... odd." She sipped her wine. "I hope you two aren't offended by how quickly I eat. I'm an only child, but I still usually out-pace everyone I know."

By a power of will, Tamsin kept a blank face. "No worries, we've been known to eat quickly as well."

Paige nodded solemnly. "You can't shock us with your eating, trust me."

The first course was cleared away, and the second plates were served. Chicken and mashed potatoes. Paige's brow rose. "I don't usually love white wine, but it is chicken ... and free. Shall we give it a go?"

Sarah nodded. "I'm with you on that." She reached for the bottle and poured. They all tried the white wine and everyone's eyes widened. It was surprisingly sweet.

After putting the glass down, Sarah gazed at the wine. "I may like this better than the red, and that never happens."

Tasting the food, Tamsin realized it was the most tender chicken she had ever eaten, and the potatoes were smooth and seasoned with an expert hand. She slowed down her bites to try to figure out what they'd used. *I wonder if I can recreate this.*

The meal finished with an apple torte and ice cream.

Tamsin leaned back in her chair, satisfied with how good the meal had been. "So, you said you worked for a nonprofit? Tell me about it."

Sarah finished her apple torte. "We work to help people with disabilities. My boss is amazing. I love my job."

She dropped her hand, and Tamsin saw a cat walking through the open-air dining room. She knew the animal wouldn't come to their table, though it seemed happy getting attention from the other guests. Sarah didn't seem too upset about not catching the furry critter's attention.

Though their bus only had them and the ten other tourists—an even dozen—there were three tours traveling together at all different levels of guidance. As the three of them sat and got to know each other, others got up and snapped photos of the scenery.

Paige took out her phone and scrolled through the photos she'd already taken. "We could easily take hundreds of images of today alone, and we're on vacation for a couple of weeks! My phone's going to explode by the time we get back to the States."

Sarah laughed. "Isn't that the point of all this?"

Tamsin could listen to her English accent all day long. They were on their first full day, and she had two full weeks of French and then English accents. She was beyond excited for what was to come.

Chapter 3 – Always Look Up

After lunch, they took another harrowing trip through small towns and twisting roads until they made it to Versailles.

The road had narrowed to one lane, and a car came towards them. Both Paige and Tamsin snickered as they sat back and watched. Both drivers figured it out, but Tamsin was again happy to just be the passenger.

Paige leaned over to look out the front of the bus window. "Can you imagine driving a car down these roads, much less a bus?"

Tamsin laughed. "Think of these roads under a foot of snow!"

"Snow, crazy drivers, and all the tourists. They could sell tickets."

The castle of Versailles had been the home of many famous people, including Marie Antoinette. Outside the castle gates, where massive numbers of people waited to enter, the tour guide pointed out the location of toilets. Feeling the discomfort and need, Tamsin and Paige ran. The line was ... well, Great America had nothing on the tight, hot hallway full of people waiting for the four stalls.

By the time they got back to the group, their allotted time was a bit past. They joined the throngs of people trying to get in the group entrance and waited. There were at least a half-dozen groups and theirs had to be the smallest. Tamsin knew there were pickpockets all around, so she held her backpack close, Paige standing right behind her. They'd brought the bag as a souvenir and it was great for a hands-free experience. But better with someone able to watch your back.

When they were finally waved in, they went through security, and then their amazing tour guide began to speak. Each room of the castle had a painted ceiling. Most had either a reproduction of the original furniture and fixtures or, in some cases, the original pieces. In each and every case, the guide knew all about it. She spoke about the intricacies, the history, and brought it all to life. She was fantastic.

If they'd gone alone, they would've never known the history of the ceilings. Some showed the images of gods, the royal children, and the different kings. A full armoire, which Tamsin thought was for clothes, had been for Marie Antoinette's jewelry. The guide showed them two different guard rooms. She explained the number of courses for each meal, that three parties were held a week and were required attendance, even if people visiting Versailles weren't feeling up to one. Tamsin stared wide-eyed at the dance room, the throne rooms, the bedrooms with their endlessly tall ... everything.

Their guide knew too much. She explained everything, from the cold hard facts to the theories, to what she felt was the truth. In the end, they got their tickets to visit the gardens at a quarter to five.

With their feet aching from being on them all day, Paige and Tamsin walked as fast as they could, their new friend Sarah right behind them as they made it to the garden and did a quick circuit. It was breathtaking. A maze of trees, manicured flowers, and a pool with fountains. There was another, small side garden with statues of animals. Each thing they looked at was more impressive than the last. As they took a final look at the gardens Tamsin sighed. "I really wish we had more time to be out here. There are fewer people and it's beautiful."

Next to her, Sarah nodded slowly. "I totally agree."

When they finally got to the parking lot, the bus was nowhere to be found. There were several dozen other buses, but not theirs.

"Did it leave without us?" Sarah's words echoed Tamsin's worried thoughts. "The guide mentioned leaving without us at the Monet gardens."

Paige looked at her watch. "I *think* she was kidding. Anyway, the bus leaves at a quarter past five, we have five more minutes."

Tamsin pointed when she saw the others from their group. "Over there."

They made their way over to the group. No one knew where the bus was, including the guide. She was on the phone making calls. They ended up waiting another ten minutes for the driver, who only spoke Spanish, to come to pick them up. Despite that, they were dropped off near the Eiffel Tower at about six.

They swapped contact info with Sarah, who kissed their cheeks before heading off. She'd been an excellent addition to their adventures for the day.

Paige turned to Tamsin, "I am so hungry. Let's grab a cab and head to the restaurant."

"It's a half hour away. Are we sure we want to go there?"

"Hungry!"

"We're by the Eiffel tower. I'm sure there are places near here."

Paige just gazed at Tamsin, hunger in her eyes.

Tamsin smiled. "Right. I'm tired and hungry, too. We're next to a hotel. Why don't we go in and ask them for recommendations."

Inside they found a concierge who gave them the names of a few places. They ended up walking a block and a half to the Café Fleur. Tamsin ordered steak tartar. The waiter made sure she understood that meant the meat was raw. Clenching her jaw, Tamsin suppressed a growl. Paige ordered duck confit. For dessert they ordered crème brûlée and chocolate cake.

They were three miles from their hotel. Tamsin decided to download the Uber app to her phone. The confirmation text wouldn't come through. Despite both of them being tired from walking all day, they started to walk towards their lodgings as they struggled with the app. It was nine-thirty at night, and people were everywhere—playing soccer, eating at restaurants, walking, biking, meeting up with friends. It felt like hours earlier. The sky was still bright.

Paige watched a group as they ran out onto a field to start up a game of soccer. "It is almost ten at night, right?"

Tamsin shrugged. "It's also almost the longest day of the year. You know, just because we're ready to turn into pumpkins, having started our day hours ago, doesn't mean they are."

About two miles later, they gave up on the Uber app and caught a cab, collapsing as soon as they got to their room. Tamsin pulled Paige into her arms. Wherever Paige was was home. She was tired and didn't have energy, but a kiss didn't take energy.

Several minutes later, Paige turned, tucking her back to Tamsin's front. Spooning, they cuddled until they were both asleep.

Chapter 4 - Mix And Repeat

The next morning, Tamsin woke before Paige, still holding her wife in her arms. As a professor at a university, she was used to rising early to get to class. Paige worked as a freelance reporter and kept her own hours. Tamsin had laid out her outfit so she could quietly dress and slip out of the room.

On the main floor, level zero, she found a continental breakfast and a machine that made any type of coffee one could want, as well as hot chocolate. She debated a double espresso but decided to stick to regular coffee. *This is good, delicious even, but it isn't up to what Orin makes.*

There were platters of ham, salami, Brie, and other soft cheeses, fruits. On another table were eggs, hard boiled or scrambled, beans and bacon. Then the breads: a hard loaf that in California she'd call French bread, she wasn't sure what they called it here ... maybe pain normal? Croissants, both plain and with chocolate, and sliced bread. On a side table were cereals, and jars of everything from jelly to honey, mayo, and ketchup.

Then along one back corner, was a two-gallon jug of Nutella. The mind whirled! Tamsin smiled thinking of how much Paige would love that. She'd probably try to eat the whole thing. She took out her phone and snapped a photo for her wife. Tingles of joy traveled down her back at the thought.

She sat with a mug of coffee and tried to wake up before she dug into her breakfast.

After enjoying a few hours of eating and reading an eBook, Tamsin headed back to the room. Paige was up. "You should've come back earlier. I didn't really want to sleep in this late."

"Sorry, love. I'm used to giving you time."

Paige shrugged. "We're in Paris."

"That's fair." Tamsin flopped onto the bed. "It's late morning, I've had four mugs of their coffee, and I'm still tired."

With a wicked grin, Paige straddled her. "I can wake you up."

Tamsin groaned deep in her throat. "You think so, do you?"

"We're alone in this huge bed, in a hotel, without a pack of family who can hear us. Really, I don't know that we have a choice." Paige ran her hands up under Tamsin's shirt, lightly rubbing her breasts with her thumbs. "It's our moral imperative, no?"

Warmth and desire surged through Tamsin despite the cool temperature of the room. "Who am I to disagree with my wife?"

Paige pushed her shirt up, and her hot mouth replaced one of her hands in a slow seduction. The slick tongue circled then flicked Tamsin's nipple while her hand continued its ministration on the other side.

Tamsin arched up, needing more contact. Her breathing got rough as Paige's teeth scraped over her sensitive skin. Then her hand and mouth switched sides, continuing the pleasure.

Once Tamsin was all but senseless, Paige lifted her head. "You, my sweet-tasting wife, are wearing too much."

Trembling with need, Tamsin slipped out of her clothes. She kept all her attention on her gorgeous wife who did the same in a slow strip tease. Tamsin didn't take her eyes off the beauty as each piece of clothing was stripped away.

Finally, Paige smirked. "Lay back down so I can have *my* breakfast."

"You know," Tamsin purred, "you could straddle me. We could both have some fun."

Paige shook her head. "Oh, no, this is my seduction."

Unable to do anything but follow Paige's directions, Tamsin laid back down on the bed. Paige kissed and licked down Tamsin's stomach until she reached her sex, and there she hunkered down.

She slowly licked up the center, twirling her tongue around her clit. At Tamsin's moan, Paige's fingers began sliding in and out in a slow exploration.

Tamsin shivered as tingles of need shot through her body. Paige continued to slowly flick and lick with her tongue. Tamsin groaned and arched as the orgasm built within her.

"That's right," Paige said, her voice husky. "Scream for me, love."

Paige's mouth descended, and she sucked, her tongue moving faster. Her fingers matched the speed. Tamsin's body writhed with need. Then she called out as a wave of pleasure overtook her.

Once she had her breathing under control, Paige had moved up to lie next to her. Tamsin rolled so their legs were intertwined, rubbing their most intimate parts together. Leaning in, she kissed

Paige, stroking her velvety skin until her hand reached her perfect breast.

Lightly flicking the nipple, she continued to gyrate atop Paige as her breathing got choppy. She gave Paige's nipple a final rub before letting her hand glide down to Paige's clit. Her wife was close, so very close. It didn't take much to push her over.

Continuing to kiss, inhaling Paige's screams of orgasm, almost did Tamsin in.

Afterwards, they showered together. Though the area was almost too small to fit them both, they figured it out, laughing and slipping against each other's slick bodies to ensure they both ended up clean.

The plan for the day had a car picking them up for a driving tour of the city. The tour began at three-thirty, so they had time to relax. They took a few moments to enjoy their downtime. There was about a half-hour before breakfast was taken down, so they headed for the main floor and the two-gallon jug of Nutella.

Once the driver arrived, they sat back as he showed them his favorite sights around Paris. He had a list that the tour company had sent. Neither Tamsin nor Paige knew what the items were on it, and as time ticked down the driver explained the number or stops would take two days. They merely shrugged it off.

Tamsin leaned forward. "Chose the places you think are the best."

The guide nodded and took the next turn at top speed.

"Would you like to get out here for a photo?" he asked at the government buildings, monuments, statues, everything.

Over and over, Tamsin looked to Paige who gave a small shake of her head. "No, thank you." She finally leaned into Tamsin. "We can get a book of professional images of all these landmarks. I have gotten so much history. I just like seeing it. Is that awful of me?"

"No, love, not even a little." Tamsin scooted closer, wrapping her arm around her.

"Very good. To your left is the palace where Napoleon slept," the driver said as he crossed several lanes of traffic from the right lane to turn left. A few drivers honked, but by now, Tamsin was used to this. There weren't many lane lines on the road. It all seemed like organized chaos that only the native drivers understood.

"We'll end by the Eiffel Tower, right?"

Tamsin looked at her itinerary. "Yes, I think so."

Paige searched their app. "What about the boat tour?"

The driver gazed at them through the rear-view mirror. "Boat tour? I was told Eiffel Tower."

"Don't worry, we'll figure it out."

"Okay, good," he said. Tamsin watched as motorcycles flew between the car and the truck next to them in the tiny amount of space. Suddenly, there was a full third lane, and the driver took it. Ahead of them were a dozen motorcycles and a few bikes. People slipped between the cars over the crosswalk.

Paige shivered. "I would not want to drive here. It's insane."

As Tamsin watched, the road opened up to several lanes. She wasn't sure how many because there weren't lane lines. Probably too constrictive for the Parisian drivers. A few minutes later, they could see the Eiffel tower where the driver dropped them off.

Tamsin gave the driver a tip and he drove away. She turned to Paige. "He was good, but I prefer the other people who've driven us around."

Paige nodded. "His English wasn't as strong." She frowned. "History has never been my favorite subject, and my head is full."

"Well, we have a long night ahead of us." Tamsin smiled. "Dinner?"

They found a steakhouse a block down the road. They sat outside and enjoyed the live music playing. Tamsin ordered steak and Paige got the fish and chips.

Afterwards they headed back for their tour of the Eiffel tower. It started at almost eight at night, and though that seemed late, the sky was bright, and the place was packed with people of all ages. They took the first elevator to the second floor, went up a flight of stairs, then waited in line to get up to the top. Circling the highest ring, they could see all of the city. The day was clear, and they could see a lot of Paris, though with the number of tourists, getting to the edge of to see out was a struggle. Tamsin thought she could smell the old leather smell of a black witch, but with all the people, and leather bags, she figured she was imagining things.

They made it out of the Eiffel Tower park area at just after nine. Navigating the tourists and people selling wares was a whole other matter. Every few feet, there were people, mostly men, selling light-up Eiffel towers, hats, buckets with wine or beer, sparkly toys, umbrellas, artwork—you name it, they had it.

They finally made it across the street and down a set of stairs to the waterfront. The last thing on their Paris list was a boat tour, which left every thirty minutes. They made it to the ten p.m. launch. Paige gazed at the line. "Why are there so many people ... everywhere? Don't people sleep?"

Tamsin pointed her phone at a QR code to get the tour narrated in English. They debated sitting on the top deck, but there were so many people, they opted for the lower seats. The tour circled the River Seine for an hour. Everywhere they went, the water's edge was lined with masses of people. The group up top yelled at the spectators on the bridges, and those on the bridges hollered back.

It was a party. Paige shut off the app with the tour guide within minutes. She smiled wanly. "I'm all historied out. It's very pretty, and still light at ten-fifteen, but no more history!"

Tamsin slipped her arm around her wife – *wife!* – and sighed. "We've been on two tours today and had two yesterday. It's our second day of French history. Just enjoying the ride sounds good to me. Tomorrow morning, we head off to London on the train."

"Hmm." Paige hummed. "More fish and chips, *and* I'll understand the language. Sounds amazing."

"Have you enjoyed Paris?"

"Absolutely. The city of love *with* the woman I love. You gave me a last name I can cherish, you know. Coming from foster care, I never felt connected to my family name. Now I have yours ... you've given me a family."

Tamsin tightened her hold, warmth filling her at Paige's words.

Once off the boat, they made their way through the throngs of people and caught a cab. For some reason, all the roads near their hotel were blocked off. The cab dropped them off just under a mile away. As they walked, they passed a building fully guarded by the police, a street party, and way too many people to be partying on a Wednesday at midnight.

The hotel door was locked. Tamsin sighed, tired and ready to be done with this longest day of the year. After ringing the doorbell, they were let in. The man with the key spoke a bit of English. He explained it was the festival of music celebrating the longest day of the year. Not all weekday nights were such a party, but he was glad they got to experience it.

Back in their room, once again, they collapsed, too tired to do much more than kiss and sleep.

Chapter 5 – Boss Level

Thursday, at two-thirty in the morning, Tamsin's phone rang. A lone wolf had invaded Santa Cruz and was wreaking havoc. They hadn't checked in, they hadn't done any of the things a lone wolf was supposed to do when entering an established pack's territory. Gritting her teeth, Tamsin debated stomping across the pond and giving this jerk a piece of her mind.

Cyrus, Bexlee, and Wynn, three of her pack wolves, were at the police bar when the man had barged in causing a scene. All three of them had smelled the wolf on him. He hadn't quite created a big enough ruckus to get arrested, but it was big enough for werewolf intervention.

Tamsin handed her phone, with Bexlee and Wynn on the line, to Paige, and picked up Paige's phone to call Georgette. While Tamsin was away, Georgette acted as alpha. She didn't have alpha-level power, but she was close, and she commanded the respect of all the other wolves.

Georgette's amused voice came through the line. "Fearless leader, halfway around the world, I take it you've heard about our tiny issue. What time *is* it there, anyway?"

With a snarl, Tamsin said, "Two-thirty. We got in after midnight, and I'm tired. I thought you were handling all this shit."

Georgette just laughed. "He's on the police's radar. Cyrus and Bexlee are trying to keep him out of jail. Having pack wolves on the force was a brilliant plan, boss." Tamsin bit her tongue as Georgette continued. "We have a few options: run him out of town, challenge him, or push him into doing something really dumb and getting arrested. A wolf behind bars isn't great, but he'd probably be there until you two get back. Then it'd stop being my issue. I kind of like that plan."

"For fuck's sake, I don't think him being in jail is a good option. Do we know anything about him?" Tamsin rubbed her temples. Beside her, Paige massaged the back of her neck.

"Apparently, Toby went to college with him. Toby says the guy is a real ass. He's gone out with Bexlee to tell him he's in pack territory. A brother-sister power team! Toby thinks he can get the guy to leave ... Bex will hang back in case it gets ugly." There was a pause and then she said, "You're off to London in like twelve hours, right?" Georgette sounded distracted. She had their itinerary on her phone and was probably checking it. "Yeah, that's right. Okay, go back to sleep. I'll text you with updates until we're asleep, and let you know when we're awake. It should be before you leave Paris. You'll be at that Gard du Nord, probably waiting in a line."

Tamsin laughed. "Waiting in line" was the subtitle of their vacation.

Tamsin woke up before Paige, as usual. Breakfast called, so she headed down for coffee and food. She noticed as she headed to breakfast that it was sprinkling outside. *Well, we avoided the rain on our tourist days. At least today is a travel day.*

Once she had her first mug drunk and was sitting with the second, she pulled out her phone to see the updates promised to her.

Toby had met with the lone wolf. The man had come to Santa Cruz to hang out at the beach. Apparently, he'd gotten a new job and had a month before it started. He wanted to blow off some steam. Not being a pack wolf, he didn't pay attention to which cities to avoid. He promised to leave town in the morning. Toby stayed with him to ensure his exodus. Bexlee had returned to report to Georgette.

Relief filled Tamsin. She didn't want her honeymoon marred by a death. She knew it could happen, but it wasn't the memory she wanted, even with all the stories of royalty losing their heads on their tours. Those events were in the past, not the present.

After her plate of food, she headed back up to find Paige awake. "Time to pack. We need to be ready to get to the train station."

Paige yawned. "I need to shower and eat."

"Shower, pack, eat, leave." Tamsin ticked items off one by one.

"Sounds like a plan."

Everything was completed by eleven when the cab picked them up. The rain had picked up, as if Paris was sad to see them leave. The drive was no scarier than all the others, with the car sliding around corners, nearly taking out bikers and pedestrians. Other drivers cut them off as they tried to get to their own destinations.

By some miracle, they made it to the train station in one piece. Tamsin wasn't sure how the Parisian cars weren't all beat up.

Paige leaned over. "Driving here is like the boss level of a game. I'm not even at an advanced level yet!"

Tamsin snorted. "I don't know many Americans who are, love."

She leaned over to give her wife one last kiss in Paris.

Chapter 6 – But The Tardis is Blue!

The train from Paris to London was blissfully uneventful. Tamsin and Paige stood in line to get their passports stamped. They waited in line to get their luggage scanned, then sat in what felt like a holding cell for two hours for the train to be ready for boarding.

"It's like an airport but much more chaotic, isn't it?" Paige observed as people got in line almost an hour early to get on a train with assigned seating.

"It is. Would you like to get a sandwich while we wait?"

"Yes! I'm hungry, and we have over an hour. Those people are here for the earlier train."

They dragged their luggage into the food line and waited. Just like in most places they'd been, the predominant language they heard was English. The descriptions of the food were written in small print right at the counter, so there was no deciding on what to eat before you got to the head of the line.

Once they'd ordered, they found seats and used their bags as tables. Both seats and tables were in high demand. Near them sat a woman from Boston, Paige started to trade stories with her. She'd moved to Paris some twenty years ago and married a local. They'd had kids, who now lived in London.

Paige leaned forward, eyes alight with mischief. "Do you drive in the city?"

The woman laughed. "Never! I make my husband drive anywhere we go. These Parisians are a different kind of driver. When we go back to Boston, my husband says the driving is so relaxing."

Tamsin just shook her head.

Eventually their train was announced, and they got in line. They stood for a good twenty minutes before the line started to move.

They stuffed their bags onto the luggage rack before finding their seats. Though the announcer eventually announced the food cars, eight and nine, open for business, neither Paige nor Tamsin felt the need ... or like moving from their seats.

The French countryside enchanted them. They passed solar and wind farms, as well as wineries and other more common farms. Homes with red roofs dotted the landscape. It took some time to arrive at the channel. Once there, the train dipped down, and everything went dark.

Paige sighed. "I guess we don't get to watch the fishes, do we?"

"No swimming with them, either." Tamsin laughed, bumping shoulders with Paige.

Once on the other side, they made it to the London train station and disembarked quickly. Tamsin looked around. "Huh, no customs?"

Paige's bottom lip popped out. "I was hoping for another stamp!"

People rushed all around them. There were arrows for taxis, buses, and the underground. After a short discussion, they headed for King's Cross underground. A search on Google maps told them to travel to Victoria station. They circled, navigating through crowds of obvious tourists pointing to the buildings, and natives scurrying to where they needed to be. They finally found their hotel, The Clermont.

Paige pointed. "Look, if we'd gone out a different exit, we'd've gotten here faster!"

Tamsin sighed, "Tourists!"

Inside the hotel, a grand staircase met them, splitting halfway up to the left and right. The receptionist checked them in and explained that everything in the room was included. "Feel free to help yourselves. We'll restock it all!"

Unlike in Paris, the bathroom was a separate area. They had more room. Tamsin thought back to the ride in from the Paris airport and the driver who warned them that everything in Paris was small. "Well, we're not in Paris anymore."

They headed out to walk. On a corner, they saw a red phone booth with the words 'Wi-Fi' on top. Paige giggled. "I thought the boxes were all blue."

Tamsin shook her head. "Those were the police boxes, not the phone booths."

"Oh, yeah. Duh! Where are the police boxes? I want to see a Tardis." She swung her head back and forth.

"Uh, back in nineteen sixty-two, probably."

Paige laughed, photographing the phone booth, despite it not being blue. Tamsin smiled, warmed by what Paige thought was photo-worthy on their trip.

They found an indoor market near the hotel with a bunch of restaurant fronts and a bar with lively music. It had the look of a food court, but the food was good—really good. Most of the people felt local, as if they made a quick stop after work to grab a meal and a drink before heading home.

They both wanted ribs, which were sold in pairs, and each pair was larger than four or five ribs back home. Being hungry werewolves, they also ordered barbeque brisket poutine. While they waited, Paige headed to the bar and returned with a couple of drinks. Hers was a Porn Star – pineapple juice, passion fruit purée, and vodka. She brought Tamsin a Margarita.

By the time they finished eating, they weren't sure they could eat the artisan baked donuts they got at a small shop at the end of the market. Luckily, the pastries were put in boxes, and they could bring their treats back to the hotel room for later.

Chapter 7 – The Long And Winding Road

Georgette had scheduled a private eco-friendly tour of London for them. It started at Trafalgar Square, where Tamsin and Paige waited for the guide. There were other tours leaving from the same area, but theirs was just them and their guide.

Eco-friendly meant a walking tour. A six-hour walking tour. The tour began at ten.

An older gentleman of Indian descent approached them. He was probably in his sixties. "Hello! I'll be your guide. We should be done by seventeen hundred, seventeen-thirty at the latest." *If he's been doing this for awhile, he probably knows everything about London. This will be a very thorough tour ... again.*

Tamsin did some quick math. So ... five-thirty. Paige leaned over and whispered, "That would make this *more* than six hours, right?" Ten plus six equaled four in the afternoon. Even Tamsin, an English professor knew that. So, yeah, more than six hours.

Tamsin smiled and shrugged.

The guide continued. "Let me know if you want to stop at any point. Otherwise, follow me. We'll be off at a brisk walk."

For a hot minute, Tamsin's heart sped up at the words 'brisk walk,' but once the gentleman started to walk, she realized keeping up with him wouldn't be an issue.

From Trafalgar square, the three of them headed to The Mall. The road near Admiralty Arch to

Buckingham Palace was mostly closed off to traffic. Both sides of the street had crowd-guards up. As they walked, their guide pointed out statues and homes, explaining the historical significance of each.

Paige slipped her hand into Tamsin's. "Maybe we should buy some of the homes near our place for guests. Then we could hold bigger parties." When Tamsin gazed at her, her eyes twinkled with mischief.

The changing of the guard would happen at eleven, and they needed to get to the palace and in position before then.

On their left, St. James's Park was beautiful. Manicured lawns and paths with people walking hand in hand. People and birds, even the Canadian Geese, looked happy.

Paige leaned over. "Are the cobra chickens in the park? That's terrifying."

Tamsin covered her mouth with her free hand, muffling the snort. "The people don't look like they're avoiding the geese."

The guide shot her a glance. "Why would they? Geese are so nice."

It took a few minutes for Paige to stop laughing. "It's like in that book we read with the girl who had to turn into a panther to get away from the geese. They're so mean in America! Nice? That's unheard of."

After that, they focused on getting to the changing of the guard. It took some maneuvering through crowds of people and the maze of blocked passageways, but they ended up at Victoria Memorial. The statue in front of the palace allowed for them to see what would eventually happen with a bit less of a crowd. There weren't any people in front of them.

As they waited, Tamsin wrapped her arms around Paige, who stood in front of her. "Have you noticed that since we left Paris, we've stopped hearing any English?"

Paige leaned back, almost melting into her. "Funny, no? All the English was left in Paris."

At just before eleven, the new guards were led by a band through the streets to the palace. Then at eleven, another band led more guards to a secondary location. Everyone who chose the Memorial to watch had to stay until the guards in the palace were released several minutes later.

Tamsin, Paige, and their guide, finally allowed to leave the center area, walked around until they found themselves at the changing of a horse guard. It was a random find but fun. Both Tamsin and Paige held back so as not to spook the animals.

Navigating the crowds, the guide eventually led them past Downing Street to Big Ben. It was just past noon, and there were thousands of other tourists battling the streets to get a picture of any statue, sign, or monument. Throughout their time with half the people in London, she and Paige tried to stay connected. Having the touch of pack helped with all the scents, sounds, and emotions around them. Tamsin could feel the tremors in Paige when they pushed through the thicker packs of people. *As nice as this is, I do miss the safety of the car during our driving tour. I'll have to make sure to tell Georgette.*

The next stop was lunch. "We need a cab. Give me a moment, I'll get one for us." Their guide was so convinced he could find one in the masses of people, cars, and buses.

After several minutes of failure, Paige suggested she could strip naked and throw herself into the street, since all were passing them by.

Tamsin took a moment to imagine the image, then shook her head as she threw her arm up. A cab stopped and she smirked at her wife. They got in and the guide told the driver where to go.

The cab, a green one, an electric car, took them to McMullen, The Old Bank Of England, which had been converted into a pub. True to form, Paige ordered fish and chips, as did the guide, and Tamsin selected meat pie. They all got chips ... big, fat, meaty fried potatoes. The fish and chips came with peas; both Paige and the guide had the option of fresh or mashed, and they both chose the former. The food was amazing.

After lunch, they walked ... There were some alleyways that took them to historical sites. Ye Olde Cheshire Cheese, an establishment that had been rebuilt in 1667, its origins ... well older than anything in California today. There were places where Shakespeare had written, and Dickens had met up with his blokes.

Paige pointed into a bar. "Maybe we can come here tomorrow, and we could do some writing. We could both claim to have written with the greats!"

Tamsin closed her eyes and sighed. "Gods above, yes. Let's do it. That sounds amazing." She took a picture with her phone so they could find it again the next day.

The guide was already heading to the next stop. Everywhere they went was rife with history and stories.

They ended up in St. Peter's Cathedral. Paige whispered softly, "Do you think we'll be struck down? I mean, we're not only a couple, we're *married!*"

Tamsin snickered. "I guess we'll have to find out."

Since lightning didn't strike them down, they enjoyed the beauty of the place.

From there, they wound their way through the streets and alleyways to London Bridge, learning that, at one point, heads on stakes had lined the entrance to the bridge, warning people of the penalty for breaking the rules. Then they walked to the Tower of London.

Finally, seven hours after meeting the guide, they sat ... collapsed. Tamsin was in good shape, but the older gentleman who ran the tour never sat and always smiled. He was a machine!

After he left, she and Paige found a truck selling ice cream with cookies and chocolate bits sticking out of the top. They bought one each and then contemplated their feet. They had an hour and a half to meet the alpha of the London pack and weren't sure if they could move.

Chapter 8 – A Pint is a Pint The World Round

The London underground was warm, overcrowded, yet easy to navigate. It took almost no time to get to Piccadilly Circus, the meeting place the London pack's alpha suggested. They arrived early, so they decided to sit on the statue in the center with many other tourists, people-watch, and wait.

A young teen set up a portable microphone and started to sing to the crowd. A separate group sang and danced down the street in traditional Middle Eastern garb, and across the circus, handing out paraphernalia, were other groups in matching outfits. Everyone had a song to sing, a message to tell, or a story to share. The joint cacophony meant it was easy to tune it all out as white noise.

Groups of people came and left. Tour guides in bejeweled and fancy bikes with attached carriages containing carpeted bench seats for passengers—their next target—to take on a quick ride.

Through all the mayhem Tamsin and Paige sat and watched, letting their bodies relax from the day. It took about an hour for the wild scent of wolf to reach them. Tamsin looked up and saw a punk-looking woman with blond hair approaching them. Her wide smile was a balm in the sea of chaos.

They both stood and made their way down the steps. If it wasn't their normal quick gait, then no one could blame them. A seven-hour walking tour would take it out of anyone ... well, maybe not their guide, but Tamsin was convinced he wasn't completely human. At the bottom of the statue, they reached the alpha and hugged. Tamsin had never met Haydee face to face, but they'd spoken over the years. They were of a similar age and had been pen-pals when they were younger.

"Tamsin! You finally made it to this side of the pond and to my city." Haydee's joy at seeing them overtook the noise of the area.

A warmth filled Tamsin as the British accent washed over her. Despite having been in London for a few days, she and Paige had stuck to tourist areas where most of the people either spoke with an American accent or didn't speak English at all. "Haydee! It's good to finally see you in person." Tamsin pulled the other woman in for a second hug.

After they separated, Tamsin took Paige's hand. "This is my new wife, Paige." She experienced a little thrill at speaking the words aloud. "Paige, I'd like to introduce you to Haydee. We've known each other from a distance most of our lives. It's about time we've met formally."

Haydee smiled. "Right now, shall we find some food? Do you like Chinese? China town is just down the way."

Paige's smile grew. "You do know the way to a girl's heart. Absolutely."

They swerved and weaved until they turned a corner and found a street lined with Chinese lanterns and union flags. Haydee turned to Tamsin. "I know this place; not terribly touristy, but the food is excellent."

"Sounds perfect."

They walked—well Haydee walked, Tamsin felt like her gait was closer to a trudge—to the hole-in-the-wall restaurant. The food was similar to what was found back in California, though not exactly the same. As with most of the food they'd eaten so far, it tasted sublime. From there, they headed out for dessert. They wandered through Leicester Square until they happened upon a Ben and Jerry's ice cream shop.

Paige snorted. "We cross the pond to get American ice cream?"

Tamsin shrugged. "Why not? At least it isn't McDonalds or Burger King, right?"

Paige scoffed but shrugged in agreement.

They sat and continued to catch up. Haydee and Paige hit it off famously.

After ice cream, they wandered until they found a pub. Despite it getting to be late, no one wanted to end the night.

Tamsin sipped her local beer and hummed in approval. She turned to Haydee. "Tell me about the pack here."

Haydee shrugged. "I have a good lot. We live just north of the city; the city proper is too expensive and crowded. There's an even dozen of us. We aren't the biggest pack, but we're family."

Tamsin took a long drink of her beer. "We had some issues with black witches over the last year. Have you had anything like that around here?"

"Witches?" She shook her head slowly. "No. There's a coven up in Cambridge, but we don't have many dealings with them. I've heard that over in your area you and the witches intermingle, but here we're still pretty separate."

Paige leaned back. "Really? That's interesting. I should start taking notes. I haven't been in the know for very long. I really only understand what it's like in Santa Cruz."

Haydee gave her a welcoming smile. "You should stay with us for a few months and learn what a real pack is all about! None of that sissy American stuff."

Tamsin threw her head back and laughed. A few passersby stared at them before moving on. "This old fight again? My pack is fantastic, I'll have you know. It's not my fault you're too scared to come see how I run my group." She waggled her hands and winked at Haydee at their old standing joke.

It was Haydee's turn to guffaw. "You just keep telling yourself that, my friend. You still haven't spent time with us either. Maybe you both should spend more time here."

Tamsin shook her head in amusement. "Maybe one day. I'm too new an alpha to be taking that much time away. But just wait, one day I'll show up on your doorstep and you won't know what to do."

"Party, I imagine." Haydee sipped her beer. "What are your plans for the next few days?"

Tamsin leaned back. "Nothing much. We had our tour today, but we have some free time now to do our own thing." She let her hand slide under the table to squeeze Paige's thigh. As much fun as she'd had touring the land, she was looking forward to some downtime with her wife—*wife!* She had to bite back a giggle of giddiness.

"Come run with my pack. You need to unwind from being around all these strange people and strange smells. Come to our pack house, run in the woods, spend a day with your own kind. It'll be good for both of you."

The idea sounded sublime. Paige's eyes lit with hope. Finally, Tamsin nodded. "I think that sounds perfect."

With that, they finished their drinks and realized the time—well past midnight. Though Tamsin and Paige could take the train to their hotel in twenty to thirty minutes, Haydee had a longer ride on her hands. They decided it was time to leave. After final goodbyes and a plan to meet for a joint run, they separated.

Chapter 9 – Exploring New Territory

A warm mouth pressed against hers. Tamsin moaned and slipped her arms around the soft, lithe body hovering over her. Soft kisses trailed down her neck. Tamsin let her hands stroke the expanse of skin down to the taut ass, squeezing it. One hand stayed to appreciate Paige's assets while the other moved around to investigate.

Above her, Paige gasped as Tamsin found her clit, tickling it with feather-light fingers. Paige bit down on the junction of Tamsin's shoulder and neck, purring softly in appreciation.

In a quick move, Tamsin hooked her leg around Paige's and flipped them. Paige squealed in delight. Then Tamsin slowly kissed down her wife's neck, past her collarbone, to her luscious breasts. She slowly circled the mound with her tongue, taking her time to appreciate its perfection. When she got to the nipple, she scraped her teeth over the tight, sensitive nub, pulling up as Paige arched, following her motion.

As Tasmin started ministrations on the other side, she let her hand drift down Paige's well-toned stomach to continue to explore and play between her legs.

She mirrored the motion she made with her tongue with her thumb as she slowly tasted her way to the tip of Paige's nipple. When she reached the peak, her thumb flicked back and forth as her teeth gently clamped down. Beneath her Paige trembled, panting with need.

Tamsin began kissing down Paige's abs as she let her fingers precede her mouth, sliding into Paige's slickness. Her fingers slowly glided in and out, Paige's heat and need evident from her writhing and small, breathy cries.

When Tamsin reached her goal, she left one hand on Paige's belly to keep her from bucking Tamsin off and lowered her mouth. She slowly licked up the center of Paige's sex, tasting the salty excitement of the morning. As her fingers probed in and out, she let her tongue circle and flick Paige's clit, much as she had done to her nipples but faster.

While Paige squirmed and her moans grew louder as she approached climax, Tamsin added more pressure with her fingers as well as a bit of teeth. Her hand on Paige's belly migrated up to play with her breasts. She sucked, licked, and flicked her tongue until Paige screamed out her orgasm, arching up, before falling back down on the bed with a satisfied groan.

She gazed down her body. "I know we're visiting that pack today, but can't we just stay in bed and play?"

Tamsin hummed in thought. "That does sound lovely, doesn't it?"

Once off the train, someone from Haydee's pack met them. There wasn't a person holding a board inscribed with their names, just the scent of wolf.

Tamsin walked up and smiled. "Hi. I'm Tamsin, and this is Paige."

The other person, a tall woman with sandy hair, dark eyes, and a no-nonsense attitude, tilted her head. "Hi, I'm Ellis. I'm to take you to Haydee."

She led them to a small car, and they were off. The drive didn't take long, but the traffic all being on the wrong side of the road still seemed odd.

At the London pack house, the group all stood around outside. Haydee met them at the car. "I thought you'd like to run first. I know how frustrating travel, crowds, and people can be. A good run can help you loosen up and relax."

Tamsin could kiss the woman. "That sounds perfect." Over the years, living in Chicago, Tamsin had learned that it was hard to hide her alpha-level power while running as a wolf. She knew it would be dangerous to run with another pack. Back in January, an alpha-level wolf had run with her pack and had accidentally pulled two of Tamsin's wolves to her. Tamsin was certain she could control that, but only because she had Paige with her: her pack, her mate, her wife. More than that, Paige was one of her submissive wolves. All that combined to mean she could run with another pack with control.

Haydee smiled as if she could read her mind. "I'll ask that you run a bit behind us, but we should have a good time."

It didn't take long for the group to strip and shift. Haydee was a large, beautiful, yellow wolf. She was stunning in looks and power. Tamsin understood why the group followed her.

They took off around the large pack house. In the backyard was a large, wooded area across a private field. The pack ran in silence until they entered the shade of the trees. Stretching her legs, Tamsin wanted to howl her joy. She waited until some of Haydee's wolves let loose before she sang with them. The new and exciting scents of the British trees and flowers filled her snout. They didn't smell like home. Even the slightly damp air itself seemed foreign.

Paige stayed between Tamsin and the pack. It wasn't that she didn't trust Tamsin's control, it was just that having the buffer helped. They also left a dozen feet between them and the tail end of Haydee's pack.

Tamsin could smell rodents that reminded her of home: pigeons, squirrels, mice, and rats. There was some bigger game—deer mostly. She could scent the trail from a few days ago ... maybe even a week. Nothing worth chasing was recent.

Paige veered left. When Tamsin trotted after her, she found the path of a family of feral cats. Tapping Paige's rear end with her nose, Tamsin reminded her mate of their goal. It wasn't discovering all the secrets of the land.

With a sneeze of understanding, Paige got back on course.

They let the breeze flow through their fur as they scoured the countryside. Paige connected with Tamsin. *"You know, I read that there aren't any wolves in the greater London area. We better not be seen as we run."* She snorted as they darted forward to catch up with the group.

"Since we've howled, I imagine we're in a safe place, love."

She howled as her pleasure flowed back to Tamsin.

The heady perfume of deer filled the air. At the front, Haydee stopped, turning to face Tamsin. She flicked her snout to the left, then she ran to the right, her pack following.

Tamsin and Paige found a small game-trail to the left. Within moments, they ran into a deer the size of a dog, but it wasn't a baby. The creature barked at them, sounding like bloody murder, then it ran to attack.

The game was on. Tamsin went left, Paige right, and they shortly caught the small deer. It was quick but small and didn't take long to bring it down.

Once they'd eaten their fill, Paige ran to find the others to see if any of them cared to join them. It took some time for Paige to return with two wolves. The power emanating off the lead told Tamsin that the first wolf must be Haydee's second, a wolf that would never accidentally switch alphas. Though Tamsin knew she couldn't attract these wolves to her, she and Paige were done with their catch, and happy to leave.

They followed the trail back to where the two groups separated. They laid down with their full bellies and placed muzzles on their paws to wait. Tamsin leaned into Paige, sharing her warmth as they rested.

It took some time, but then a dozen wolves dashed by.

Not in a hurry, Paige and Tamsin rose and took off in the same direction as Haydee's pack. They shortly got to speed, finishing their time on four paws and enjoying the day.

Back at their clothes, they shifted.

With a huge smile, Paige asked, "What did we take down? It looked like a miniature deer. I've heard of miniature horses but never deer. It was cute, though it barked; was it a dog? I mean, it barked bloody murder, or it was dying. So, what *was* it?"

Haydee's eyes widened as Paige spoke, her words tumbling out almost too fast to understand. Finally, when Paige seemed to run out of words, the pack facing them looking to be holding back their laughter. Haydee said, "You found yourself a muntjac deer, our very own barking deer. They come from Asia, but they are definitely a variety of deer. We found a red deer." She pointed at the woman who'd picked them up from the train station with her chin. "Ellis wanted to thank you for sharing."

After everyone was dressed, they all headed inside for wine and socializing. They planned on staying late, and probably heading back the next morning. A day with wolves in the middle of their honeymoon full of strangers had helped to center them.

Chapter 10 – The Enemy of My Enemy ...

Tamsin woke up alone. *Paige must be in the bathroom or down having coffee with some of the pack.* They'd gone to bed late.

Her mate ... *wife!* ... didn't often wake before her, but it wasn't unheard of. She shook her head, determined not to worry on their honeymoon. Tamsin pushed herself up and stumbled to the ensuite. She took a quick shower then put on the clothes she'd brought for the day: jeans and a graphic t-shirt with a large phoenix on it flying up towards the shoulder.

Down on the main floor, in the kitchen, Tamsin poured herself a large mug of coffee. The only other person in the room was Ellis. Tamsin sat next to her. "Who else is up? Have you seen Paige?"

Ellis sipped her coffee. "As far as I know, we're the only two up. I haven't seen anyone else come through here, and from the kitchen I can see and hear anyone come down the steps."

"How early do you get up?" Despite the warmth of the mug she held, Tamsin's hands went cold. *That can't be right. Paige couldn't have just disappeared.*

"I usually get up early. I have to be in the city by seven and it's an hour by train. I tend to get up early on the weekends as well." She shrugged.

Dread washed through Tamsin. "Paige isn't upstairs. Where else could she be?"

The other woman's face stiffened. "I don't know. Does she normally wake up early? Does she wander off? Maybe take a run?"

"No, she usually sleeps in. She isn't a morning person. I was surprised she was up, actually." Tamsin started speaking faster as she explained this to Ellis. "Should I be worried?"

Ellis stood. "I'll rouse the pack. We'll do a sweep. I'm sure we're both putting the cart before the horse. With the time difference, she probably just got up to take a walk before I woke up."

Heart beating faster, Tamsin nodded. She placed her coffee on the table before mumbling, "Yeah, that makes sense. Thanks." She liked her lips, deciding maybe it was something else ... some *one* else. "I'll be back in a moment." She ran up to the room. Getting down on her hands and knees, Tamsin started sniffing. Near the bed, she found what she was seeking, the scent that shouldn't be there: old leather. She growled.

Back in the kitchen she found Haydee. "It was the fucking black witches."

Haydee shook her head. "We don't have them here."

"In your pack house? The Greater London area, or Great Britain?" One of Tamsin's brows rose in challenge.

A snarl vibrated from the alpha. "Anywhere around here."

Tamsin's jaw clenched before she forced out the words, "You do, and they took Paige."

"How do you know?" Haydee's eyes narrowed. She didn't seem to be doubting Tamsin, just curious. For the longest time the theory was that black witches didn't have a scent. It was only during the past few months that Tamsin's pack had figured it out.

As Haydee's wolves joined them in the kitchen, Tamsin explained what had happened in Santa Cruz and how they'd discovered that black witches had a distinctive scent. "It isn't as strong or obvious as regular witches, but it's there. If you smell the floor near the bed, you can just pick it up."

One by one, the wolves went to the bedroom to get the scent. From there, they shifted and headed out, searching for any clues they could find. Tamsin wanted to help; it was a need burning deep in her gut, but she didn't know the territory and she realized she would be more of a hindrance than a help. It irked her more than she'd've expected. A burning fire of irritation.

She paced the house—first the living space inside, and then the grounds outside. The tension in her body made her want to howl. Her fingernails bit into her palms, drawing blood, and she forced her fingers to unclench. She shook out her arms and tried to relax her muscles.

It didn't take long for her to have to repeat the process.

After what seemed an eternity, Haydee came out to give her some news. "One of my wolves found the trail. Ellis and I went out to follow it with him. It stops about two kilometers out. We think she was put into a car."

Tamsin turned in the direction Haydee had come from. "Show me her path. Maybe I can find something. Are you friends with any of the local witches?"

Haydee's face hardened. "We aren't like you lot in the U.S. We don't work with witches."

"Working with witches may be the only way to find her. If I have to, I'll call in favors from home. I'm sure someone from the local Santa Cruz coven knows someone here."

"We take care of our own, Tamsin." The alpha sounded pissed ... as immovable in her anger as a brick wall.

Tamsin wasn't much happier. "You may take care of your own, but not taking any advantage at your disposal is just silly. I have some of Paige's stuff. We can utilize that to find her ... *if* we use the witches. The black witches must know you won't go to your common enemy. Well, *I* will."

"My pack can't support you if you insist on working with the witches," Haydee spat out.

Taking a breath to stay calm, Tamsin nodded. "I understand. At the end of the day, I have to know that I've done everything I can to save my wife. Werewolves are smart, strong, and powerful. When we work with witches, we are that much better."

With a snarl, Haydee glared at her. "If you will not be swayed from this foolish path, I will work with you. There is a chance my second, Ellis will too. But, Tamsin, I won't ask the rest of my pack to work with witches. That's asking too much of them."

It felt like a weight had been lifted from her shoulders. Tamsin needed to find Paige, but she was in a foreign land. "Thank you."

Haydee sighed. "We need to get to Cambridge, and I don't know if they'll work with us. The animosity is real."

Tamsin ended up calling Cinthia, the coven leader in Santa Cruz. While Cinthia made a few calls on Tamsin's behalf, she took the train back into London, packed up their room, and traveled back to Haydee's pack house. She didn't think they'd be returning to the hotel.

During that time, Cinthia's efforts yielded fruit: the name of the coven leader in Cambridge: Jazmine. There were other covens around, but she was a powerful witch and willing to help.

Like the wolves, the witches in the UK didn't want to intermingle with the other supernaturals. The fact that they found one person to help was something of a miracle.

Tamsin, Haydee, and Ellis decided to take the train to Cambridge. It was faster than driving. If they ended up needing a car, Tamsin would rent one.

Outside the train station in Cambridge, they saw a statuesque woman with long, dark, flowing hair that reached her waist. Bright blue eyes found them in an instant. Despite the loose white blouse and patchwork skirt, Tamsin could see her whole body stiffened.

Jazmine walked up to Haydee and reached out a hand. "Haydee, it's been a spell."

"Jazmine." Haydee held herself stiff. Ellis stood a few feet back, scanning the area as if another witch would jump out and attack them.

"This way." She waved them on. "I have a car. We'll be off to a private park area." Jazmine went on to explain that there was a central coven house, but she didn't want to give that location up to any of the wolves. "I need to do a scrying spell. I have all the materials I need with me, save something that belongs to the wolf who is missing."

"Paige," Tamsin said sharply.

"What?" Jazmine shot Tasmin a quick look.

"The wolf who is missing is named Paige." Tamsin used all her skill as a teacher working with misbehaving students to keep herself calm. "I get that you don't like werewolves, but my aunt was a witch, and I grew up with witches and wolves getting along. One of my wolves is a member of the local coven, a born witch-wolf hybrid. It's different where I come from. We are more than just civil, we are friends, mates, and a community. The *person* you are looking for is named Paige, and she is my wife."

Jazmine's face softened. "I *am* sorry. This idea of community between our peoples is foreign. I will help you find your wife. I don't believe your conviction will do anything for the schism between the alpha of the pack and me, however."

Haydee's mouth tightened into a line, but she didn't disagree.

Tasmin sighed. "Fair enough."

When they reached the wooded area, Jazmine set up her spell, taking Paige's hairbrush. Haydee, Ellis, and Tamsin all backed up and let Jazmine work. After a few minutes, she made some marks on a map she'd laid down on a rock. She looked up at Tasmin. "It looks like they've taken your wife to Edinburgh. They may not stay in that location. There's an international airport there, but for now, that's where you'll find her."

Tamsin nodded. "Thank you. We'll be on our way."

Jazmine's mouth tightened into a flat line. "There are black witches in my territory. If you'll allow it," she turned to Haydee, "and if *you'll* allow it, alpha, I'd like to join you on this trip. I can be useful, and I'd like to eliminate this blight from our lands."

Chapter 11 – A Trip Up North

Despite it meaning Jazmine traveled with three wolves alone, she opted to not involve any of her other witches. The four of them piled into her car and started the drive to a hotel. "The only trains up north will leave in the morning. Our choices are to either drive or wait."

Tasmin squirmed. "Is driving an option?"

"It's a long drive; over six hours. We'll have to take turns."

Haydee and Ellis both nodded. Haydee leaned forward from the back seat. "We can each drive. I think only Tasmin can't drive with their backwards American driving."

Jazmine sighed. "Okay. I'll need to get some things packed, both spell components and clothes." She gazed in the rear-view mirror and slumped. "Can I really trust letting you two know where I live, or should I drop you off somewhere and pick you up afterwards?"

With a dramatic sigh, Haydee dropped her head back. Then she rattled off an address, presumably where Jazmine lived. "We're werewolves, not savages. We have access to modern technology. It's not like we're going to come after you. What are you afraid of?"

"War," Jazmine stated simply.

"Well, we're not after any type of war. We just want to live our lives. We have jobs and families, just like you. And unlike you, we don't have any ranged weaponry."

Jazmine's jaw dropped. "We'd never start the fighting."

"Then there's nothing to worry about, is there?" the alpha replied gently.

The car pulled up to a row of flats. Everyone but Jazmine stayed in the car as she jumped out and ran into one that looked like all the others. After a few minutes, she returned with a bag ... a very big bag.

"We should get off here. The price of the petrol is cheaper." Jazmine scrolled through her phone, not watching the road.

"No." Haydee's ire filled the car. "I know where I'm going. There's a good pub in fifteen kilometers. We can get petrol and food there."

"Sounds good to me, boss," Ellis said, voice light, but supportive.

Jazmine sighed. "That's fine, we can get food there, but the petrol costs quite a bit more there.

We can save several pounds if we stop he—" The car flew past the stop. "Never mind."

"Ellis, have you called your friend?"

She checked her phone. "Yeah, we have reservations at a hotel: Ten Hill Place in Edinburgh."

Jazmine sighed. "That's in the middle of a fairly touristy location."

"And we're getting a deal, so what does that matter?" Haydee snapped and shifted to the left lane to pass a truck.

"It'll be harder to do my spells away from nature." Tasmine could feel her frustration.

"You said," Haydee shot a glare at the witch as she looked over her shoulder to merge back into the right lane, "that you could do the spell anywhere."

Tasmin growled low in her throat. "We've been in this car for four hours. We have at least three more. Are you two going to snap at each other the whole time?"

There was a silence before they both mumbled 'no.'

Ellis checked her phone. "We'll have two rooms. How do we want to split up?"

Tamsin rubbed the bridge of her nose. "They couldn't get three?"

"No, we're lucky there were two."

"Well, I'm fine with the three of us piling in a bed together. I'm used to doing things pack style, either in wolf or human form."

Haydee smirked. "Works for me."

It was late by the time they arrived at the hotel, and they all agreed to start the search the next morning.

Edinburgh was enchanting. After another hotel that served an amazing continental breakfast-- America had a lot to learn--they were off. The streets were full, but Jazmine had done another scrying and found out that Paige was being held near Edinburgh castle.

Tamsin debated counting the pubs they drove past, but realized she wasn't sure she could count that high. They rounded a corner, and at the top of a street that rose was the castle. On either side of the street filled with people were shops selling cashmere ... everything. Knickknack shops with souvenirs, a woman playing a bagpipe, two other women holding out owls for people to hold or pet for five pounds, and pubs, lots and lots of pubs.

The group swerved and twisted around locals and tourists trying to get to wherever it was they had to go. Tourists gaped at shops and historical buildings and all the varieties of liquor and then bought stuff. *Paige would love this.* Others stopped randomly to snap pictures, everyone walked in the wrong place, confused as to which side was the correct side, and the smokers ... so many smokers. *Paige would growl at the smokers, probably without even realizing she was snarling.* Ever since landing in Paris, the scents almost destroyed Tamsin's nose and Paige had been growling at all of them.

They may have been able to pick up the scent of a witch or wolf if the air wasn't so saturated with cigarette and vape smoke.

The road grew skinnier ... or maybe it was just more people crowded the area, as they approached the castle. On their left, they passed a whisky touring museum. Tamsin debated coming back for that with her wife. It may be more interesting than most of what she'd seen. And if they offered samples ... she shook her head; she had to stay focused. Her eyes misted as she imagined Paige by her side, where she should be.

They went around, past the pedestrians, to a side area, an alley between buildings out of the sun. Trying to breathe slowly, to calm herself, and to catch any wayward scents, Tasmin finally caught it, the slight wild scent of wolf: Paige. She started walking in the direction she could smell it. She wanted to run, but there wasn't room.

A hand fell on her shoulder in a vise grip. "Tamsin, what are you doing?"

"Can't you smell that?"

Haydee shook her head. "What?"

Ellis came up next to her and breathed in deeply and slowly through her nose. "Got it boss."

Haydee nodded. "Find her."

In a deliberate loping walk, Ellis took off. Tamsin went to follow, but Haydee snagged her arm. "One person can jog off and no one takes notice. A group will cause an uprise. Ellis has an excellent nose. Trust in my people."

It felt like barbed wire being dragged under Tasmin's skin as she forced her head up and down in a nod of agreement. *How can I trust anyone to find my mate, my wife? It should be me searching.* She felt heat on her cheeks and realized the tears that threatened before slid down her face.

She hadn't recognized she'd taken a step until Haydee's hand landed on her shoulder. "Please, Tamsin. Ellis knows this area, these people, everything. You are a stranger. It will go much smoother if you trust us. Let us be your pack."

Haydee wrapped her arms around her in a hug. "I understand, my friend. We'll find her."

Biting back the growl, Tamsin shut her eyes and let herself cry.

After a bit, she stepped away from Haydee. Jazmine came over and wrapped her hand in both of hers. The touch was warm and comforting. "Welcome, Tasmin, to our land. We hope nothing but peace for you and yours. Though the worst has happened, me and mine will do what we can to make right what has gone wrong. Tranquility be yours as we walk this path."

The words, ancient in their meaning, washed over her. They were different than any she'd heard spoken in Santa Cruz, but this was a much worse situation. Exhaling, Tamsin nodded. "I enter in peace and hope for nothing but tranquility for you and yours." She bowed her head, trying to let the familiar phrases do their magic. She needed the power from the exchange to let her think. If she stayed stressed, she'd be of no use to any of them.

Jazmine smiled and placed her hands on Tamsin's temples. "And harmony be yours."

With those words, Tamsin finally felt a rush of cool calm rush through her. "Thank you."

A few moments later, Ellis returned. "Her path leads to the east. I'm not sure why they came this way. The scent of old leather got thicker; I'm guessing they had more of their clan waiting up here. They gathered them up and are traveling somewhere else. Again, their path ended when they most likely got into a car."

Haydee nodded. "We need to regroup and get something to eat. Hungry and running wild we won't do anyone good."

All of Tamsin's muscles tensed. She didn't want to give up ground.

Jazmine placed her calming hand on Tamsin's arm. "They are in a car driving. I can't scry until they arrive. Food is the right path forward."

There was an eating establishment down the street from the castle that smelled divine, The Deacon's House, Scottish Café. Tamsin ordered tomato and basil soup with sourdough bread. It was just what she wanted as the rain started to fall. As she ate, she sent up thoughts to all the gods she'd ever heard of. She wasn't religious, but at this point, she'd do anything to get Paige back. *Please let her be safe ... bring her back to me.*

They headed back to the hotel, and Jazmine headed into her room to scry again. "She's at the airport. I don't know where she's headed, but they're leaving the country."

Chapter 12 – Visiting More of The World

The plane ride was short, but that didn't change the fact that they were in a puddle jumper ... literally. They were jumping the water between Scotland and Ireland. It only took about an hour and a half, but the plane was tiny. It was also filled with Americans.

Next to her, Jazmine shook her head. "I may be the closest thing to a local around. So many of your people on this plane."

Tamsin laughed. "You're not wrong. It's like everyone decided to take this trip today. On the bright side, we're the only two of our kind on this popsicle-stick of engineering as well."

Jazmine sighed. "It's rather unfortunate that Haydee and Ellis didn't bring their passports when they followed you to meet me. They were so convinced we'd catch up with your mate in Scotland, it didn't occur to them we may need to fly elsewhere."

"But it did to you?" Tamsin narrowed her eyes at the other woman.

"I have a healthy lack of trust. I'm just always prepared for anything ... just in case."

Tamsin laughed. "I can understand that." *I like this woman. I wish she and Haydee got along. I think if they could get over whatever caused the division between witches and wolves in this country ... or their country, they'd realize they had a real ally.*

The propellers on the plane spun, the vehicle taxied, and they finally were in line to take off. It was a much smoother ride than Tamsin would've expected, including the landing in Dublin.

Once they disembarked, they took a cab to the main drag. From there, they found a random hotel and they each got a room. Tamsin threw her and Paige's bags in, putting a few supplies in her backpack before finding Jazmine. In her own room, Jazmine had pulled out the implements to scry. At this point it was almost second-nature for her. They found Paige near Trinity College. Since the hotel they'd found was located near the college, they headed out on foot.

They crossed the River Liffey and followed the streets towards the college. It was summer, so classes weren't in session. The campus was filled with a bunch of tourists.

As they got closer, Tamsin knew it didn't feel right. They found another side road that wasn't too populated, and the witch did another scry. Jazmine pursed her lips. "They've moved over to Merrion Square, a park a block or so over. They're on the move, let's go."

They circled to the south of Trinity College, then followed along the to the east until they got to the park. Tamsin felt Paige's pull. She reached out. *"Are you okay?"*

She felt the frantic struggle give way to a deep calm. *"Tamsin, are you really here? They put something over my eyes, and I think I've been on a train, a plane, and an automobile. I didn't think you'd find me. Neither did they. There's something they want from me and since I'm not from the UK or an alpha, they figured I was easy prey and wouldn't be missed. I was going to shift and run, but until now, I've been in cars or locked rooms. I didn't think it would help."*

Tamsin's face went hard, and she spoke out loud as well as to Paige. "You did the right thing, and of course I would find you. And they were wrong. You are neither easy prey nor expendable. We are coming for you, just hold tight."

Relief and love flowed to her through their bond. Jazmine smiled.

Tamsin asked if Paige knew how many black witches there were. Paige had heard three different voices, but figured there were more. "And their scents are so similar, it's hard to tell."

After Tamsin filled her in, Jazmine's face scrunched up. "What do you think our options are? Should we try to fight?"

"There are a lot of them. This won't be easy. We have surprise on our side. If I'm a wolf, it'd help, but we're in a public place." Tamsin let her mind ruminate for a moment. "It would be better to slip off with Paige and have you and the pack come back later and take care of this group. We can grab some of their items so you can find them again. I didn't come on my honeymoon to clean up international messes."

Jazmine grunted. "I don't like leaving them here, but you're right. Grabbing your wife and getting away is our best bet."

They found where the witches were setting up, near the center of the park in a copse of trees. Paige was in the shadows, with two women sitting on either side of her. Three others were circling the area.

Two walked near. Tamsin and Jazmine were hiding in the shadow of the trees and Tamsin could hear them because of her werewolf hearing. "I don't know why we're doing this out here. Why don't we go to the coven home?" the younger one with straight blond hair asked.

The other woman with wild red hair shook her head. "If there's any chance we've been followed, we don't want anyone knowing that location. This is private enough. It's rainy today, no one's out just hanging out at the park. We're fine."

The blond sighed. "I don't know, the whole getting wolf powers without becoming a wolf ... it sounds like a fairy tale. I'd think I'd be just as happy being a wolf."

The redhead slapped her friend. "Don't let anyone hear you speak like that. We're witches, and powerful ones at that ... black witches. We can do anything we want. You'd lose everything if you turned furry, probably your brain as well."

Paige snorted. "We have a few wolves who can do magic. For being the brainy ones, you sure don't know much."

The two gaped at her. "You're lying."

"Nope. No reason to. Two of my pack mates can do spells and a wolf from another pack as well. You are way behind on information." Paige smirked. "But, in my neck of the woods, the wolves and witches get along. None of this awful animosity you've been going on and on about. It sounds dreadful."

Jazmine leaned over. "What are her bindings? Can you see her?"

"No, we aren't close enough, but they're rope."

"Oh, so they're not metal." Jazmine looked up towards the tops of the trees. After a moment of nodding, as if she'd been debating a point, she said, "If I burn them, how much damage would that do to her?"

Tamsin snarled softly. "Too much. Let's work on getting her out without long term damage. She can turn wolf and slip out easily enough."

"What about her clothes?" Jazmine almost sounded scandalized.

"Well, it'll be fun to watch." Tamsin said, mouth twitching.

She sent Paige what she wanted and a basic image of where she was. Tamsin was correct, they'd assumed the blindfold and confusion about where she was would be enough.

The shift from human to wolf wouldn't take long, so Tamsin told Paige to wait until the witches were off on one more round to check security. Apparently, they wanted to start their ceremony at exactly fifteen hundred, or three p.m. *Whatever! It works for me,* Tamsin thought.

At just after two-thirty, the group did a final check before setting up. The park was clear, and Tamsin gave the go-ahead.

Paige shifted. Getting out of the clothes took a bit longer than they'd hoped, but clothes rip. The blind fold fell away, and Paige ran. The three of them ran two blocks to St. Stephen's park. They cut through the trees and bushes, hiding as best they could. On the far side they found a deep, dark place for Paige to hide.

Tamsin dug through her bag for clothes for Paige. It was some of the emergency items she'd thrown in her bag. Paige shifted, slipped on the jeans, t-shirt, and shoes, and smiled. Tamsin pulled her into a hug, then clasped her face and kissed her. It felt like it'd been ages, and she almost lost herself in the action. She had to remind herself they weren't in a safe space and pull herself from Paige.

Tamsin sighed. "Not enough time, we need to get out of here. We're still in the fire."

Jazmine flagged down a taxi. They all got in and headed back to the hotel. There, they debated leaving for the airport, but the likelihood the witches would attack again that night was slim. First, they'd have to find them, then they'd have to break into a well-established hotel when their target was aware this time. All in all, they felt safe enough. They'd leave the next day.

As they separated, Jazmine gave Tamsin a quick hug. "It was great meeting you. I dream of a day the witches and wolves here get along as they do in your city. I'll leave you two lovebirds to enjoy the last night of your honeymoon. Tell Cinthia I'll talk to her soon."

Tamsin smiled wide. "It was lovely meeting you, as well. Thank you for all your help."

Back in their room, Tamsin got on her phone and purchased two tickets for Chicago leaving in the morning. She was happy to actually find a flight on such short notice. Then, keeping to the highly populated areas, they carefully selected a pub and had a fantastic final meal.

Paige smiled. "One more place to try fish and chips."

Tamsin lifted her glass. "But this time we add Guinness!"

Chapter 13 – All Good Things Must Come To An End

After dinner, Tamsin called Haydee. Haydee sounded concerned. "Did the witch locate Paige?"

"Yes, *Jazmine* found where the black witches were holding Paige, and we got her back."

"You did? I would think there would be some news of the fight. Did you keep it quiet?"

Tamsin sighed. "We got her away without them seeing. With two of us and at least four of them, the battle wouldn't have gone well. In all honesty, the only way you'll get rid of the group is if you and the witches all work together. If you look at any historical records from my country, the only time full black witch covens have been defeated is when wolves and witches work together."

A snarl reverberated through the connection. "You're not going to change us, Tam."

"I know. There will be animosity forever, yay animosity," she rolled her eyes, "but that doesn't change the fact that you have a problem. The black witches know that America isn't safe for them, and you lot won't work together. Just remember, the enemy of your enemy, and all that."

Close to Haydee, Ellis snorted. "What if we think we can do it alone, without the spell-flingers?"

Paige knocked her shoulder into Tamsin, amused by all of this. She knew how asinine they were all being. "Then you may succeed, but how many of your pack are you willing to sacrifice for your hubris?"

Someone gasped in the background.

Haydee growled again. "Fine, I'll speak with my pack. Black witches on our land changes things, especially since they came into our home." She paused for a beat. "Do the witches have a protection spell for that?"

"I don't know, but you could ask them."

Once they got done discussing witches, they enjoyed rehashing the run and discussing Haydee possibly visiting Santa Cruz. They exchanged a few more pleasantries, and Tamsin thanked her and Ellis again for helping track down Paige. It didn't take long for their conversation to come to an end.

At breakfast the next morning, Tasmin and Paige ate with Jazmine. They continued their discussion about the black witches with her over the elaborate continental offerings. It seemed all the hotels knew how to feed their guests.

Jazmine sighed into her tea. "There were enough of them that we will need the pack, won't we?"

Paige put some Nutella on a chocolate croissant. "They have power and have been living unchecked for too long. Your groups working together really is the best bet."

Tamsin told Jazmine about how the black witches had been going around the U.S. trying to take down packs and covens who weren't working together, ones they saw as weak. "The power we have working together is beyond even the strength they get from death. It's our ace in the hole. If you can find a way to get your people to work together, then you can clean house."

Jazmine guffawed. "You make it sound simple, my friend."

"No, not really. It took years of struggle for the witches and wolves to find common ground, and it's still hard for many of our people. But it all started with two groups working together. You have a chance, here and now, to make a difference."

Jazmine sighed. "I know that my coven can't take on the black witches alone. Using our magic, we can do a lot of things, but we can't defeat that many of them.

If the pack is willing to work with us, I think I can get my coven to see reason and work with them. Even if it's just for this one deed."

Their flight to Chicago—their new fight—left at nine in the morning from Dublin. It arrived just after eleven. They were planning on spending a couple of nights there to end their honeymoon away from other wolves, witches, or black witches. Tamsin still had her apartment; she hadn't given it up. She figured if any of the pack needed to come out this way, it was a great stopping place. And now, it was perfect for them.

They tried to sleep on the plane, knowing that time would be way different back home. Once they landed, they gathered their stuff and took the L, the elevated train, into the city towards the apartment. It took a transfer, but they made it eventually.

After a few quick calls to their pack, the Chicago pack, and the London pack, letting everyone know they were safe, they took a walk to a local café. They were both tired, and UK time said it was time for dinner, not lunch, but they needed to adjust back. They ordered coffee and cake and found seats.

After they ate, they turned towards Bucktown, wanting to stretch their legs.

Tamsin turned to Paige. "You know, after everything, being back here, I want to run. Do you want to run?"

Paige's eyes lit up. "I'd love to run."

It didn't take long to get back to Tamsin's old stomping grounds from when she used to live in Chicago. It felt like she was coming home, though this wasn't her home anymore.

They shifted and started their run.

The wind tickled her face, the leaves and branches scraped her muzzle, the scents of the woods filled her snout—she ran. Feeling the pull of the moon, running through the woods, and hunting...Tamsin loved everything about being a werewolf. The scents—the woods, the wet soil, the animals around her—called to her senses.

The series of sharp yips sounded from her left. She stopped and lowered herself into the long grass. Tamsin lifted her nose and sniffed. Paige, running and playing in the grass.

Connecting with her wife, love and happiness blossomed between them. She howled to the moon, then sent to Paige, *"Having fun?"*

"I am." She ran up and tackled Tamsin. *"And you know what else?"*

"What?" Tamsin picked herself up and snuffled out a laugh.

"I love you, Tamsin Hath. And I am happy you are my wife."

She darted off and Tamsin followed, hot on her trail. *"I love you too, Paige Hath."*

Have you missed any of Coastal Wolves? Find the full series here!

https://mybook.to/Sv1tM

Where to Find Harlowe Frost
Thanks for reading!

Find more of my books on my website, including you can buy

signed books**!!**

http://hannahwillowauthor.com

You can also find me on:

Twitter: @hannahwillow217

Instagram: @hannahwillow217

Facebook Hannah WillowFacebook: Harlowe Frost Author

About the Author

Harlowe Frost has been a teacher at both the high school and college level. Her parents instilled a love of reading from a young age. She grew up in the queer community. Her favorite genre growing up was fantasy and science fiction, that is, until she discovered urban fantasy and paranormal romance. What she never found in those books was the diversity in background, gender identity, and sexuality she saw in the people around her. She decided if she couldn't find that in what she read, then she would write it herself. This started her writing paranormal romance with a LGBTQ+ background.